A CUP OF TEA AT THE MOUTH OF HELL

Also by Luke Tarzian

The Shadow Twins Series

Vultures

Adjacent Monsters

The World Maker Parable

The World Breaker Requiem

The World Reaper Odyssey

Anthologies

Dark Ends

A Cup of Tea at the Mouth of Hell

(Or, An Account of Catastrophe By Stoudemire McCloud, Demon)

Luke Tarzian

INTRODUCTION &
ACKNOWLEDGEMENTS

This book is a very short book. It includes a novelette and a brief collection of essays and ramblings about trauma and grief. Mind you, when I began writing this story several months ago, I had no idea it would become what it has.

You see, the story was conceived on a whim. One afternoon I had a thought: what would happen if someone stole Lucifer's beloved tea kettle? The title came almost as quickly (and with a chuckle). I set about drafting the first chapter of what I thought was going to be a whimsical, slice-of-life fantasy about the devil and a missing tea kettle, a respite from the far darker and emotionally harsher stories I typically write.

I was wrong. Holy shit, was I *wrong*.

I was about four-and-a-half chapters in when I mentioned a movie called *The Family Stone.* This, as it would turn out, would be the kindling of something far more personal.

A Cup of Tea at the Mouth of Hell is what I call a semi-fictional memoir, built upon the trauma of losing a parent to cancer. It is whimsical, yes, and it is funny, but it is primarily an invitation to connect. To feel and be felt. As of writing this, my editor, my beta readers, and every reviewer who's read this story, has cried.

I did not set out to write the story this book became, but I am so very grateful that Sir Stoudemire McCloud, Demon yanked the pen from my hand and took me on the introspective journey he did. I am humbled.

So take care, dear readers. Go easy on yourselves. And if you find yourselves relating to this story more than you anticipated, I would love it if you let me know. Grief and trauma are odd, vicious beasts, but they need not be faced alone. I know that, now.

Briefly, some acknowledgements. This was a very secret project for a while; only a handful of people knew about it because I was not sure when it would be finished or when I would publish it. So, thank you to Rowena Andrews, Ashley Brennan, and the clandestinely named RainyBoi, extraordinary beta readers and cheerleaders, even better human beings and friends.

Thank you to Victoria Gross, editor supreme.

Additional thanks to Justin Gross, Dan Fitzgerald, and A.C. Cross for being the kind and compassionate people they are. I am immensely grateful.

To Stoudemire McCloud, Demon:
Thanks for saving me.

"At grief so deep the tongue must wag in vain; the language of our sense and memory lacks the vocabulary of such pain."

— Dante Alighieri, *The Inferno*

"Fuck squirrels."

—Stoudemire McCloud, Demon

Briefly, A Word About Order
(Or, Welcome)

Order is the focal point around which existence revolves. Without order there is only chaos. And in the halls of Damnation[1] the first sign of impending chaos is a cup of tea made without the water having first been well and properly boiled in a kettle.

Why is this relevant, o nameless narrator? you ask. *Who cares about the preparatory order of* tea *in the fires of Hell?*

Lucifer, dear reader. After all, how does one expect to properly greet the newcomers to Hell without having first had a hot cup of tea to bulwark the cold[2]?

Behold the Morning Star, frantic on the annual Morning of Souls, the arrival of Damnation's newest recruits.

Someone has misplaced the kettle.

---

1. Pronounced *Dam-NAWT-ion*, thank you kindly.
2. The first circle of Hell is a cornfield of snow.

Act I: Sad Boys

IN WHICH WE DISCUSS THE IMPORTANCE OF TEA

"It is not *just tea*, Stoudemire."

"Actually, it is," I said, adjusting my spectacles. "By definition, things are what they are. Water is water. Demons are demons. Ergo, tea is—"

"Essential!" Lucifer massaged the spot between his eyes. He always did this when a migraine was close. "Look—yes, tea is *just tea* in the very sense of the word. But on the Morning of Souls—"

"'Tea is the flame with which we thaw the cold uncertainty of death.' I know. It was the very first thing I was told when I arrived however many millennia ago. It's also on every one of your holiday cards."

"Lest people forget," said Lucifer. His arms were crossed to his chest as was common. His wings, numerous threads of brilliance streaming from his back, flapped and hissed of their own accord. Blessed be the one who incurred his wrath today; Lucifer was toeing the threshold of rage.

I sighed and adjusted my spectacles again. "Look, where was the last place you saw it, the kettle?"

"Atop the stove. Preemptive placement—"

"'Is paramount to the perfect pour as stove and kettle must consent to the birth of sacred sip by means of acquaintance on the Morning's Eve,' I know. For the record, might we reconsider a revision? It all seems a bit…wordy. Jumbled."

"No, we may not," said Lucifer. "Simplification is the death of tradition—I shall not forsake tea as God[1] forsook me. *That* would truly be a sin."

I rolled my eyes, withholding a snort. At the very least, being secretary to the Lord of Hell was never dull. A bit flamboyant and exaggerated, sure, but never boring.

"Right. Back to the matter at hand—the kettle was last seen atop the stove. Might we return to the kitchen to look for clues?"

"Do you intend to dust for fingerprints?" the Morning Star inquired.

I narrowed my eyes. I had wanted to be a crime scene investigator prior to joining the legions of Hell; I had utterly failed.

"I shall pretend your inquiry was not in jest," I said, "and will attribute your tone to the obvious withdrawal[2]."

Lucifer was silent.

"Right," I said. "To the kitchen[3]."

---

1. Synonymous with "Asshole."
2. (A story for later.)
3. Pronounced *kit-SEE-hen*, because we apparently ignore common conventions in Hell.

In Which Our Story Fails
to Progress
(Or, a Semi-Oral History of the
Kitchen)

I f, dear reader, you at the very least happened to skim the previous entry, then you'd have noticed the Morning Star and myself referenced the kitchen. Hell, by definition, is an absurdity, so it should hopefully not come as a shock that the kitchen—henceforward known as *The Kitchen*—is more than its name would imply.

But Stoudemire, you said that tea was—

I am well aware of what I said, thank you kindly. But not everything in existence is literal —and that includes The Kitchen.

So now we have to listen to you ramble about —

9

Educate, dear reader. I am going to educate you. While what I say here in no way, shape, or form will propel our story forward, it should hopefully provide context for the madness ahead (and curse me, there is *a lot*).

The Kitchen of Hell (if memory serves me well, and it usually does, I believe the good people of New York City repurposed that name with far more sinister connotation in line) is, for all intents and purposes, the nexus of our little land below. A mixing pot, if you would—a fluctuating amalgamation of ethereal dreamscapes the mind can scarcely comprehend.

There's also a lot of food[1].

The focal point of The Kitchen, though, is a plume of scalding steam. The plume, the only one of its kind, boils the water for Lucifer's tea and is aptly called *The Stove*[2].

---

1. What—did you think a place called *The Kitchen* would be bereft of sustenance?
2. I promise *that one* obeys proper conventions.

In Which We Discover
a Clue
(Or, an Extended Manifestation of
Withdrawal)

Hell is a peculiar place, an absurdity as I've previously said. While there *are* day and night in the simplest of terms, these fluctuations in the emittance of celestial luminescence are more deeply tied to the Morning Star's health. Ergo, the happier Lucifer is, the longer the days and vice versa.

As we sojourned to The Kitchen I watched sunlight wax and wane, observed the desecration and rebirth of myriad constellations. Beautiful from a distance yes, but to anyone privy to the fact these celestial happenings were indicative of worlds destroyed—horrifying.

We stopped beneath a purple willow tree and Lucifer took a seat against its trunk. His typically golden hair had lost its luster and his eyes were circled black. I sat on a rock a few feet away, notebook open, pen in hand.

"What are you feeling?" I inquired. Secretary to the Morning Star was a deceptive simplification of my duties as also functioned as his therapist. My word, the stories I could tell[1]...

LUCIFER HEAVED A SIGH. He had been doing that more often as of late, the missing kettle notwithstanding. Everything seemed so much more...constricting, and the absence of a good hot cup of tea on The Morning Souls served only to exacerbate that feeling. Being the Lord of Hell was not easy, especially when you had demons of your own.

"Deflated," he murmured, his voice somewhere between wet gravel and day-old coffee. "Aimless."

Stoudemire scribbled into his pad. "Why?"

Lucifer raised his eyes, gently arching his right eyebrow. "It's always the same, Stoudy. Do I really need to elaborate?"

Stoudemire peered over his spectacles, lips drawn to a line. "It matters. It always matters. There are deviations whether you can see them or not. Continue, please."

Lucifer took a shallow breath but it did little to ease the tightening of his chest. It was difficult to drown one's angels when they knew how to swim, and this one had been gnawing at him for millennia despite his best efforts.

"I still dream about the Fall."

I sighed. I'd a feeling he was going to say that. Cast aside for differing views, barred from home because he'd dared to dream of something more than a life spent tormenting humans with the burden of myriad mental chains and woe.

"Paradise my wingless ass," he sighed. Over the centuries, over our many sessions, Earth and Heaven had become synonymous with one another. Rather, they had become synonymous with the concept of Paradise in so far as they were both ruled by miserable people keen on spreading misery to all (at least, this was what I'd gleaned from our many conversations as well as my own few decades 'mongst humanity).

"Do you know the worst part of it, Stoudy? A part of me, larger than I'd like, still longs to return to those golden fields. Despite everything, a piece of my heart yet remains with my blood-kin in Heaven."

I furrowed my brow, offering what I could only hope was a sympathetic smile. "I think maybe it's that way for many of us, hmm? I see this with the adopted. It's not exactly the same but I think it's the tug of the What-If. The life that might have been. In no way is it a slight toward the family one came to be a part of—just…curiosity and a tiny pang of loneliness. Does that make sense?"

Lucifer took a moment before nodding.

I adjusted my spectacles—again—and held my pen at the ready, ballpoint hovering atop my notepad like a hammer ready to strike an anvil.

"Tell me about the particulars. I mentioned things deviate almost imperceptibly—what, exactly, is nagging at you?"

He frowned, pursing his lips.

"I remember a pot of tea…"

IF, dear reader, you are wondering about this particular pot of tea, you will be dismayed to learn we stood and withdrew from the shade of the willow tree before Lucifer divulged anything more.

As I waited with bated breath, his eyes drifted, falling upon a feather. I'd noticed it earlier and thought nothing of it. However, the longer it held the Morning Star's gaze, the more fixated on it I became. At first glance it was little more than a large white feather. Upon closer inspection however, I took notice of the fluctuations in color, of the fact the feather was not so much a feather per se but rather formed of myriad tiny leaves of parchment.

"Oh dear," I murmured, and I could surmise

from Lucifer's glare we had come to the same realization.

Heaven had kidnapped the kettle.

---

1. (But shall refrain from doing so because doctor-patient confidentiality stills my tongue)

In Which I Recall My First Encounter with God
(Or, that Bastard on Broadway)

That Heaven had taken hostage of Lucifer's beloved kettle came as less of a shock than I'd first imagined it would. To understand why, allow me to provide context of the humanly sort.

Some time ago, when I was a mortal twist of flesh, anxiety, and liquor, I found myself in weepy prayer to God, kneeling in a pool of urine 'neath the summer sky on a sticky New York night. On Broadway, specifically. The ins and outs of the whole ordeal more or less escape me. However...

They say humans are of God. For the longest

time I thought that was a crock of—pardon my
tongue—shit. Were it true the world would have
been a better, kinder place. As it stands, humans
are of God. They, like their divine progenitor, are
prone to acts of malice, thievery, and violence. I
came to this realization that night on Broadway
when I first encountered God.

I blinked, my speech slurred. I was sloshed,
but not enough that I couldn't comprehend the
being which had manifested before me.

"You... You're God?"

Before I could muster another word I was
bombarded with acorns. I could only watch as a
bag of raisins was viciously ripped from my
pocket and my assailant skittered into the night.
God, I had learned, was a two-foot-tall klepto-
maniac squirrel.

So it came to be we found ourselves with a lead.
We had little, if any doubt the agents of Heaven
had absconded with the kettle. The conundrum
we faced, however, was reaching the ethereal

plane of our quarry. The angels, as you've probably guessed, are not exactly keen to welcome the citizens of Hell 'yond their gilded gates, especially not those who come with the Morning Star in tow.

"What do you think?" I asked.

Lucifer frowned. "We could… No. That won't work. Perhaps…" He glared, spat, cursed. Picked at a flake of dry skin behind his ear. I could tell he was stressed, increasingly so. Nasty business, psoriasis.

He took deep breath, held it, and exhaled raggedly. "I think… I think I need to be alone for a while. Meet me at Bean and Brew tonight."

"But you despise both of those things…"

"The taste, yes," he said. "But not the smell. Never the smell."

Lucifer withdrew.

I scribbled onto my pad.

In Which The Morning
Star Laments

The Morning of Souls had commenced as indicated by the myriad threads of illumination touching down elsewhere in the seventh circle. Good on the custodians to have welcomed the newcomers to Hell in his stead. Lack of tea not withstanding, Lucifer was currently unfit to bid welcome. It pained him endlessly; he'd not once missed The Morning of Souls.

"I suppose there's a first time for everything," he murmured, walking the woodland aimlessly. He'd had a lot of those lately, firsts. Panic attack. Vomiting blood. Hair falling out, etcetera.

Now with the tea or lack of... He'd not stopped twitching the entire day. He *needed* the tea. Longed for it. Tears welled in his eyes and a ragged sigh escaped his lips.

No. Didn't need the tea itself. The kettle, the last remembrance of his mother. Everything else...just trauma. What was it Stoudemire had said in a session some years ago? Trauma was not a memory; it was a reaction *to* a memory.

The Fall.

He tensed his jaw, continued through the woodland, soothing with its rivulets of luminescence and the lullabies of night birds settling in for their morning sleep.

Eventually, at the north-most edge of the wood he came to a lake, at the center of which was island connected to the mainland by a bridge of hovering, scarlet stones. Lucifer crossed, stopped and gazed in reverence of this sacred place to which he'd journeyed. Mortals, he knew, had revered this structure in its life for its ability to distract from the stress—and that was what he needed now. A distraction, a temporary respite from the chaos of his mind.

He walked into Blockbuster and rented *The Family Stone*.

SOME TIME later Lucifer sat at the edge of the island, gazing into the lake. He was numb; that had been the worst possible choice, The Family Stone, and now he found himself more agitated than he'd previously been. Itching. Burning. Nausea. Bits and pieces of the The Fall. Last conversation with his mother.

And a girl named Light.

Mama, I... I finally met the one.

His tongue was dry; his mouth felt sticky. He swallowed, trying not to think of tea, and fell back into the grass, closing his eyes and awaiting sleep.

Everything else could—

A SONG SWIMS across the ether, twists along a Southern California night. In an unnamed recreation center, people gather in a throng a memories and tears. A young man watches from the very back before withdrawing. If he has to listen to one more second of The Beatles' *Here Comes the Sun* he's going to crack—and he's already staring down the void.

The world is a cruel and unforgiving place, and his chest tightens the more he thinks about the unfairness of it all. The treatment was supposed to save her, not give her fucking *leukemia*.

He'd been married in April. It was October now and his mother was was dead. With her had gone a piece of his soul. At least she had gotten to see her boy married off…

When he returns home he turns on the television, unstops a bottle of scotch, and, over the course of the next eight hours, consumes two thirds of liquid amnesia.

He does not sleep. How can he when he's had a cup of the devil's tea at the mouth of Hell?

Instead, he drags himself to his bedroom, to his desk, and procures a notebook and a pen, for the misery of these last few weeks and days and hours have exhumed something, and he writes a to a girl he knew once. Her name is Eleonora and she was the worst.

If my words were but a cliché from a movie or a romance novel, then I'd be standing at your grave in Forest Lawn, where you're now presumably at rest. I'd be standing in a pair of black jeans and an achromatic v-neck t-shirt, wondering exactly what it is I meant to say. But because my words are not some chestnut from a poorly-written book or movie, I'm not standing at your graveside pondering the words I mean to say—because, truthfully, even as I write, I've still no inkling as to what it is I'm meant to say. Should I still harbor feelings wrought from hatred, sorrow, and distrust? Or should the fact you thought about me even in the months before your death instill in me the courage to forgive you for the months of psychological distress?

It's been five years since I cut all ties between us, four years and three months since you tried to talk to me again. After everything you put me through...you had the audacity to act like nothing happened. Admittedly, it threw me for a loop—the idea that someone that I really thought I loved could scar me so emotionally, tear the trust out of my heart, and then waltz back into my life as though their indiscretion was only but a dream. It was infuriating, and it only made me loathe you more.

But let's again pretend, for the sake of adding imagery, I'm standing at the door before your tomb, a rose in hand as winter coats the park of lifeless souls like bitter sand.

I'm breathing in the air, thinking to myself, "Now that I'm older, isn't it colder than before?" Why would I burden myself with such a thought, you ask? Perhaps because I feel a weight still resting on my shoulders—not a heaviness inflicted by abhorrence, but one imposed on me by guilt that comes from never saying what I felt. I've wrestled with my thoughts and dreams of you for months, trying desperately to figure out exactly how I felt. Despite the demons of your being, the corruption that neurosis wrought inside your mind, you were still a sweet and giving person, and that is some-

thing that I'll never once deny, despite how many times you left me feeling used.

You came to me a broken thing, and I did my best to fix you, worked what little magic I possess to put a smile on your fragile face—and initially you did the same for me, tried to make me see the good in things despite the fact that I was swimming in a pool of loneliness brought on by the sudden death of someone very close to me. In that sense, it was our negativity and longing for companionship that drew me to you. You confided in me things you never let your friends know, and I in you. We had our little of ring of imperfection, and that's what I adored about our closeness to begin with. We gave names to birds and rabbits and several other creatures, all of whom we claimed as children of our own—a little inside joke of ours that only made me love you more. And perhaps the thing that I loved most about you was the sincerity in your voice every time you said, "I love you."

And yet...it was what I hated most, because the only thing that I knew how to do was say "I love you" in return, despite the countless times you broke my heart. I was a reliquary of despair, and when you tell a broken person that you love them, they're inclined to believe you. I'd like to say I never knew I could be scared by something so divine, but there was never anything divine about our time together. It was just a nightmare—a sullen dream with cracks of light eventually engulfed in bitterness and sorrow.

So let's pretend I'm standing once again before a tomb, a rose in hand as winter falls upon me. And let's pretend the tomb is empty, with a plaque that bears my name.

What of that should I make? What significance does an empty tomb have with my words to you? Perhaps regret and disappointment—a certain sorrow that I dare not dwell in for too long. There was a moment in our time together when I thought we might grow old together; and when the time to move on finally came, I'd be waiting in the cemetery where our bodies dwelled, anticipating your arrival, with a smile on my face. And sadly, I can still see you walking through the snow in my direction, with the smile of soul instilled with warmth despite the chill the lack of physicality possesses.

But I'm not standing in the snow of Forest

Lawn before your grave—I'm sitting in the darkness of my room, drunk and wallowing in my thoughts. For I feel the point of writing you tonight is threefold: firstly, to accept the wrongs you did to me and the apology you issued to me on your death bed; to say that since you passed, I've done my best to hold you in a higher light because I truly do forgive you; and to reiterate how truly lonely and inferior I feel sometimes, because the embrace of the one you share a bond of physicality with is the single most idyllic feeling in the world.

HE'S TREMBLING by the time he finishes. The flood gates come crashing down and he curls up in his bed, weeping at the losses and heartache and the loneliness these last several years have brought. Abner. Eleonora. Now his mother. They always did say trauma comes in threes.

He pulls his childhood stuffed rabbit to his chest and hums the entirety of *Second and Sebring*. When the sun peeks through the blinds, he finally falls asleep.

In Which I Consult The Oracle
(Or, Stoudemire Puffs a Docbie)

I had a lot of time to kill while waiting for Lucifer to return from wherever he'd wandered off to. When we reconvened at the Bean and Brew tonight I assumed he'd be a tad more...mellow.

Hoped, rather. To assume is to make an—well...I'm sure you've heard the phrase.

I digress. I hoped by the time we next met he'd be more evened out, and the thought of Lucifer even more wound up than he currently was sent prickles up my skin. As I mentioned previously, the length of night and day is directly tied to the mood of our beloved Morning Star. I'd paid it little mind upon our departure earlier in the day, but as I wandered toward The Kitchen the fragility of his mental and emotional state was on dazzling display for all to see. Frankly, I'm shocked I didn't suffer a seizure.

By the time I reached the outermost rim of The Kitchen my own mind was screaming, so I paid a visit to a man named Glee. He ran a top-notch pizzeria, the best in all of Hell.

He also happened to be my…physician.

Soon thereafter we sat in a corner booth, consuming pie. Glee was expecting an evening rush, half to do with the questionable integrity of the cosmos, half to do with the simple fact that people liked an evening high to go with their evening slice.

He took a bite of pepperoni and bell pepper, swallowed. Took a breath and blew cerulean smoke that shaped itself to something resembling a top hat-wearing moose.

"I can imagine the poor bastard's got a lot yankin' on his chain," said Glee. Bastard, I had learned some time ago, was a term of endearment here, somewhat synonymous with the word "orphan" but more sympathetic.

"Indeed." I closed my eyes momentarily, breathing smoke of my own. A corgi in a vest. "Truthfully, I think it's less to do with the actual tea and more to do with the sentimentality of the kettle. Belonged to his mother, you know." I breathed more smoke, coughed. "The— The ritual of it all. A hot cuppa to warm the soul, to welcome the cold and frightened souls and give 'em a bit of cheer."

"Mmm. Makes sense," said Glee, "but you should stop with the Britishisms. You're from fuckin' Brooklyn and your accent is shit."

"I am properly *stoned off my tits*," I sang. "Can't be helped."

Glee rolled his eyes.

A flying fox caught wind a yard of two away. I watched it take to the sky with the amount of grace one could reasonably expect from a bat simultaneously attempting flight and aerial self-satisfaction.

I giggled. "That isn't real."

"Course it ain't." Another twist of cerulean smoke from Glee, this time in the shape of moose. "We're all blitzed. The mind does funny things when happy smoke's afoot."

"How can smoke be 'afoot'? It doesn't have feet."

"You get what I mean," muttered Glee.

Briefly, a dark room and an Ent flashed across my mind. They were superseded by a television re-run of some mindless dribble called *Jersey Shore*; beside the television stood a ficus.

I blinked.

And I ate.

WHEN I LEFT the Gleezzeria I had lost all concept of time due in part to my overconsumption of pie and the fact that Lucifer's fragile emotional and mental well-being had skurned the ty into a continually fluctuating stream of cosmic diarrhea.

I pushed my way through the throng of

teople paipsing about The Kitchen until I found a park bench upon which to lie. Beyond it sat a pond filled with quacks ducking loudly. I exhaled slowly and eyesed my close. The Bew and Brean would cait.

Si needed leep.

In Which We're All
Fucked by Absurdity
(Or, Help Me, Please)

I dreamt, and I knew it was a dream because the eyes through which I watched the world were not my own.

The sky was gray with a blanket of clouds; it rained lightly and I stood in the backyard of a house atop a hill. Gravel crunched beneath my feet and the wind whipped my jacket about.

The air boomed. My heart thrummed in a way I'd not experienced. Vibrated, almost. My eyes turned to the sky as a massive shape sailed overheard. All black save a crown of scarlet feathers and eyes like stars. The great bird ascended, disappeared briefly into the clouds before it manifested once again, thunder trailing in its wake, orchestrated by a single flap of its great wings.

"Thunder Bird," the mouth that was not mine murmured.

The dreamscape shifted yet the great bird remained. I next found myself along...well, I'm not entirely sure what to describe it as except a celestial walkway beneath which myriad worlds took shape, swayed by the flapping a thousand birds. Had I come to the nexus of fantasy? Something about the presence of the birds intrigued me, more so than the chaos of manifested worlds.

The biggest—the Thunder Bird—landed several feet from where I stood, great wings enfolding it almost like a cloak. That scarlet crown shone brighter even than its starlight eyes.

"Whence you come is a place of insecurity and woe. Ever-shifting. Such is misery." It cocked its head. "Last we met you wore a different name."

"We've never met."

"We have," said the Thunder Bird. "Like I said —misery is ever-shifting; it subtly decays the mind, rewrites memories like a virus in a lullaby."

I was no stranger to the profound. Even so, the words gave me pause. A virus in a lullaby... My spine chilled; that phrase had stirred something in me—but what?

"We will meet again," the bird said, unfurling its wings for flight. "Such is the way of things here."

Flap.

Thunder.

Fog swirled around me. Dilated to reveal a tree and a girl in white. Beyond them stretched a meadow and a sea of gray-gold clouds, the melody of a familiarly muffled song fluctuating with the severity of the wind.

The girl looked at me with coal-black eyes and I awoke on the park bench with a scream.

HEAVEN WAS an autumn-dusted orchard above which myriad crystalline towers floated. The air was crisp and Lucifer wore his wings around him like a cloak—

His *wings*.

He unfurled them, six brilliant lengths of inscribed parchment tipped with scarlet plumes. His body was of the same configuration, myriad sheafs of parchment tattooed with divinity, each glyph unique in its purpose.

He lowered himself to a crouch. With a great *flap* he ascended from the orchard and Heaven's various towers and tiers passed by like the skimmed pages of a book.

He alighted on the utmost tower in the eight-ieth ring of Heaven and the world before him was wasteland of tarnished literature and floating crystal. Leafless trees stood gnarled and twisted like the hands of someone who had died painfully.

A song drifted through the desolate air, accompanied by clockwork gears in counter birl. From the tarnished earth arose the corpse of a tower. Beyond its glass he saw a face, and it beckoned with soundless words.

Lucifer approached, but every step he took decayed his parchment form. By the time he reached the glass he was little more than a head at rest atop half a torso, legs crumbling, arms already having burnt to ash.

He fell to his knees. Out from the darkness beyond the glass rolled a green apple.

"O, weary wanderer," sang the rotten world. "Why do you torment yourself so? Why not leave the past where it is meant to lie?"

"Because," murmured Lucifer, "it's killing me. I have to know. I have to know about Light and the Fall."

"So shall it be," the world said. "But you'll not like what you find. Come, now, and we'll have a spot of tea before we enter Hell. *True* Hell."

Act II: Whimsical Monstrosity

In Which I Search for
The Morning Star
(Or, Heaven is Shit)

L ook, you've stayed with me thus far. I'll admit, this is not remotely where I expected our story to go. But such is the fucked up whimsy of Hell. Yes, it's a beautiful place but...it's still *Hell*.

I wandered for a while after rousing from my dream or nightmare or whatever it was I'd had. I made my way to The Bean and Brew on the off-chance Lucifer was awaiting my arrival, but no one there had seen him.

I returned to the tree beneath which we'd had our impromptu therapy session. Almost imme-diately, in a manner with which I am still unfamiliar, I found myself transported halfway to the other side of Hell to a grove above which starlight shone eternal. I groaned, for it was at this point in time our story transcended sheer stupidity in favor of absolute absurdity.

"Welcome, o Stoude of the Mire McCloud," said a voice not unlike the spawn of Mario and a leprechaun, "to Phallic Forest."

(If you're wondering where the forest got its name it's definitely not from the myriad cock-shaped trees. Yes, I realize I've gotten less eloquent as this tale has progressed, but can you blame me? All of this started because I tried to help the Lord of Hell find the fucking tea kettle with which the agents of Heaven had absconded.)

"Truly, I am *thrilled* to be here." I narrowed my eyes. "Would my caller consider coming forth?"

I groaned as my request was met. I'm not a fan of serpents, never have been. I'm *far less* enchanted by the existence of the bell end boas that inhabit Phallic Forest. But such is the way of things here.

I digress, and shall endeavor to spare the details of the massive, throbbing—

"Please, forgive the abruptness of your summons," said the boa. "I am called John'Son and I require aide. You are aware that Heaven has stolen our Lord's kettle, I think? There is more to it than you are aware of. Please, would you follow me?"

I had little choice and so obliged John'Son, trying my best to ignore the eggshell-white trail of mucus he left as he went and the absolute *undulation* of the forest and its inhabitants. Bit hard, no pun intended, when the entire locale is the closest approximate to a physical manifestation of a fucking tentacle-fest.

But I digress. Again.

At length we reached a marble temple in which rose an effigy of The Morning Star depicted as The Great Worm Which Split the Sky[1]. I arched an eyebrow.

"I have seen this very statue many times," I said to John'Son. "I commissioned one not seven years ago."

"This is the utmost of the effigies depicting

The Great Worm," the boa said, "gifted to us by the nomad Puce. Countless ages it has stood here, providing guidance to those in need—until today. You see, Stoude of the Mire—"

"Just *Stoudemire.*"

"—it turns out the effigy was—is—a means to plant a seed... A portal, really—"

"Between Heaven and Hell—are you fucking kidding me? Never mind the blatant metaphor you seem to be grossly unaware of... Never mind any of it. Are you telling me one could theoretically, *probably* enter Heaven by way of...?"

"Riding The Great Worm—"

"Traveling *through*—"

"—to completion? Yes!"

I blinked, taking a moment to process the sexual whimsy. Reader, I could not have wrought such a place if I'd tried, and the fact that Phallic Forest existed is a testament to the sentience and creativity of Hell itself.

"Right. Right..." I looked from John'Son to the statue and back. "I don't suppose you know where our Lord Lucifer is, do you?"

The boa nodded toward the effigy. "He is beyond."

"In Heaven? Since when?"

"Not an hour ago," said the boa.

None of this was making sense. All this hopscotching about. I shook my head; I was feeling my fatigue. To think, the day had started with a missing tea kettle...

I frowned. "Hang on—how did I even come to this forest? And how did you know about the kettle? None save the Demijarls—

—Fuck."

Away fell the forest in rivulets of scarlet and white, and in swept darkness and the hot flame of needles biting my tits.

"He's awake," said a voice like a boot stuck in mud, but wetter. "Welcome, friend. I was beginning to think you dead—and we're just getting started."

---

1. Different than that bullshit peddled by the bible.

In Which Stories are
Told and the World
Burns
(Or, I've Lost My Fucking Mind)

E verything anyone has ever told you about Heaven is a lie. I want to reiterate this as best I can, especially the part about divinity and justice. Let me tell you, O reader, there is nothing remotely just or divine about hovering over a pool of piranhas, strung up by your tits and testicles while several cherubs edge an archangel in the corner of the room to the melody of George Michael's *I Want Your Sex*.

For the umpteenth time, I digress.

I relented to the pain and shat myself, at which point the archangel blew its load and the cherubs danced in circles like the sexual acolytes they were. I breathed as best I could, but my ribs stung something fierce. My thoughts were adrift in fog; I'd no idea how long I'd been here let alone *how* I'd come to be here.

Save the aforementioned, the room was bare. No windows, no door. Clearly, it was meant to intimidate its occupants, but it was a little hard to feel intimidated when an archangel and cherubs were engaged in casting couch antics.

A voice came to me in the depths of my mind, at first like gravel in water, gradually building to a whisper not unlike the rustling of leaves in an autumn breeze.

"Do you fancy something...less?"

I... How was I to answer?

"Might we cast away the room of ecstasy for something tame? Green hills beneath a starlit sky? The pages of your favorite book?"

Um...sure?

A rustling tickled my ears; *pages turned* and I found myself before a tower black, garbed in cotton robes and cleansed of pain.

"A curious fascination with towers," said the voice. "Even more so with the Devil's mind."

"*The Morning Star,*" I said firmly.

The voice chuckled. "Call a pile of feces chocolate pie; it is what it is, as nature intended."

I ignored the slight. *Am I dreaming?*

"We are *always* dreaming," said the voice. "You will have to be a bit more specific."

I was in Phallic Forest, I said. *Then I heard a voice—not you, someone else. They'd thought me dead, said they were "just getting started."*

My phantom antagonist chuckled and in doing so stirred the sky to swirling gray, coaxed the ether's tears to fall.

"The mind is such a...*silly* place. Here—" A green apple manifested in rustling of pages. I caught it as it dropped. "Stay a while and listen. We have such stories to tell..."

TODAY I TALKED to my anger and it told me its name was Grief, writes the young man. It's been almost four years since his mother's death. The world has changed and so has he. He's become angrier, more irritable. Reactionary.

He's an author, or at least he fancies himself one. He's three books to his name and is working on a couple more when he's not consumed by debilitating procrastination birthed of imposter syndrome and fatigue. What's the point when no one reads your words? What's the point when it only makes you sad?

His first book was good, second was even better. The third? His best effort yet despite the fact it nearly drove him into therapy—*back* to therapy (did a couple months' worth shortly after his mother's death).

He should have listened, should have found a couch and impartial ear. He knows he should have—but he didn't, so here he is.

Angry.

Sad.

Alone.

Grief caresses his cheek and it feels like an evening autumn breeze. At first soothing, but quickly melancholy. Such is the way of Grief, of those chill and silent nights when *maybe* the only sound you hear is the faint rustle of dry leaves stirring memories of things and people you once loved who left you broken-hearted.

He closes the notebook, goes for a walk in the lamplit streets of his suburban neighborhood. The air smells of freshly cut grass and laundry detergent and it reminds him of college heartache.

He walks for miles. Walks to the house they used to live in, now renovated and bereft of character. He walks uphill, along a street behind the house leading to a cemetery. He stands at the gate, spellbound by rumination. There is a history to the burial ground, personal yet at the same time not. It influenced his first book, unpublished, but its occupants are nameless and unknown, as is he to them.

He can't help but smile wryly; he's standing in a scene from that very book, brooding and lamenting as a fog rolls in and the romanticized fantasy of lamentation takes the stage. Except, this is real.

"You're mistaken."

The young man starts, turns to the voice—a

figure in silhouette, backlit by a pair of lamps along the cemetery road.

"About what?"

"Fiction," says the silhouette. *"It's all real, just to varying degrees."*

"Are you real?"

"To you."

"Are you supposed to be an epiphany?" he asks. "Because if you are…" He shrugs. "I don't understand. I haven't understood shit for years." He jabs his chest with his thumb. "It's empty. It's *been* empty."

"I know. Which is why you've written your way here, to this place to which you've walked so many times. It carries memories and gives birth to inspiration."

He blinks, and he's sitting in his office chair at work, feeling light, feeling…something.

A breeze slips through the open window and it sounds like paper, like the turning of pages in a book…

STORIES, O reader, are peculiar things, and this one in particular starts in the clouds, at the Edge of Night before a sea of stars. I expected the narrative to be supplied by my phantom antagonist with the voice like rustling leaves, yet what I was presented with was a distortion of my own. I recognized my verbal intonation but the presentation had the feeling of molasses. Like a dream I'd had so many times before, in which I ran a race but every step felt weighted.

Still, I watched and listened.

There was a boy with a fishing rod who wished to catch a star, for doing so would make his wildest dreams come true. However, try as he might, he could not catch a star. He asked his mother why and she told him stars, like all things, are free-willed.

"Think of it like this," she said. "Were you a star and someone cast a fishing line into your home, intent on taking you for their own desires, would you like that very much? Would you indulge them or would you go about your life?"

The boy had never thought of it like that. The

very thought of leaving the clouds, being *taken away* from his home made him sad.

"Maybe I could rescue stolen stars," he said.

Ages passed. The boy became a man and sailed the Edge of Night, rescuing many a stolen star from people looking to capitalize on dreams. In his years and travels the boy had learned to strip a star of luster was to sentence it to a gradual and agonizing death. A life bereft of free will was not a life worth living.

When he had rescued all the stars he could the man retired to a town at the Center of Night, whereupon he found the Bookshop in the Clouds. It was run a by woman named Light, and she told the man she recognized him. Some many years ago, he had rescued a star from the charred pages of a dying book (for all stars in the Edge of Night were born of books). Her name was Light and until this day she had never been able to thank her savior.

From her apron she procured a folded piece of parchment and handed it to the man. "My story. I wrote about you, The Man Who Rescued Stars."

She touched his arm and they shared a moment of eternity, gazing into one another's eyes. Hers like the waking moon and his like gentle suns.

"I ask that you leave Night," she said. "Leave Night and see the vastness of the world. Read my story. When you have done these things, you will understand. When you have done these things, come seek me where the sun is silent."

So he did.

The story ended. The tower fell away in rivulets and I found myself amidst a ruined world, decorated by the frayed and tattered pages of a million books, their story-corpses strewn about. Fragmented crystal mottled the earth and air and my lungs stung with rot.

Before me stood the body of the tower, its skeleton at least, and on its other side I spied the gnarled and tarnished remnant of a man. *The* man.

I sprinted through the ruin. But when I reached my destination he was gone.

And I was lying in his place.

In Which the Trauma
Hidden 'Neath Our Paper
Flesh Comes Forth
(Or, Me, Myself, and I)

Beyond the glass of that dead tower, in the darkness whence the green apple had come, sat an old wooden chair in the center of a dusty, rotted room, illuminated by a dozen faint threads of light. Before the chair stood a mirror.

Lucifer manifested in a twist of shadow, limbs restored, the structural integrity of his parchment form maintained by the tower interior. He approached the mirror, his footfalls leaving splotchy ink. Each step took something of him, of his vitality, and by the time he reached the mirror he was little more than a paper mannequin, featureless and plain save holes for eyes.

He looked at the mirror, puzzled, for the visage gazing back was not his own. Pale skin, dark of hair, and brown of eyes, a pair of spectacles perched atop its nose.

Stoudemire?

The reflection stepped out of the mirror and caressed Lucifer's cheek. Its index finger found his face, tracing lightly where his mouth should be—and then it was, and Lucifer tasted the dust and rot and sorrow of the room. Next came his nose, and he wished he could not smell.

"Stoudemire?" he asked again, this time aloud, and his throat screamed for it was dry and half-formed, made partially of paper.

The reflection—Stoudemire—turned attention to the room and traced the air, hands moving as if he were conducting a symphony. Two chairs, a small table, and a pot of a tea. Two cups, a bowl of sugar, and a jar of milk. Not the fanciest of presentations but it stoked the slightest bit of comfort in Lucifer.

"Sit," said Stoudemire. "Please."

SO I SAT, dear reader, and poured myself a cup of tea. Stoudemire sat across from me and did the same. We sipped, listening to the melody of dying Heaven whisper through the cracks. Have you ever heard a blue whale mourn its stillborn calf?

I placed my cup on the table and folded my hands in my lap. "How long?" I asked of Stoudemire. "How long have I been this way?"

Stoudemire sighed. "Since the Fall. Since…"

"Since Light," I whispered.

"We find solace in stories," Stoudemire said. "We always have. But I think…I think the Fall of Light may have broken us, else how could be talking, you and I?"

He reached across the table and touched my arm. "Sometimes solace is a mask. You know this —you're the one writing these words."

My heart is racing, and my hands are trembling. Though they remain folded in my lap, I know what Stoudemire says is true. And I know about the Fall of Light—I think I always have, even from the very first page of this story.

IT IS August 2018 and the young man is numb. He sits inside a restaurant with a friend. They drink and they eat. Then, they go somewhere else, and they drink some more. This goes on until very late in the night. It's understandable.

His mother is sick.

It's leukemia.

He knows. He *knows*.

IT IS September 2018 and she has grown weak. They have her birthday in the hospital. She and his father celebrate their anniversary. Twenty-nine years married, together for thirty.

They listen to the Beatles.

It is October 2018 and the end is near. The young man is internally a wreck. He hopes, holds out an *ounce* of hope—but the doctor says they've exhausted all options.

The young man knows.

He *knows.*

He listens to *Second and Sebring* on the drive home from the hospital and he cries.

At least she got to see her boy get married.

It is October 18, 2018.

The young man's father calls.

It is October 18, 2018. It is late. It is eight o'clock in the morning and the young man has not slept. He's drunk half a bottle of scotch.

The sky is full of clouds.

He hates *Here Comes the Sun.*

Iᴛ ɪs December 2018 and I want to die.

Iᴛ ɪs July 2022 and I miss my mother, my guiding Light. I am an angry, sad young man. I am lonely and tired.

Iᴛ ɪs August 2022 and I am close to the end of this book. A much shorter book than I thought I'd be writing, but I've learned the shortest works are often the most profound. To me, at least.

I think of *The History of Love* by Nicole Krauss as I write. I think of all the times I tried to mask the voices in my head by telling myself they were just that—voices. But trauma is ever-shifting. It is not a memory but a reaction to a memory.

My reaction to my trauma is this novel that become a novella that became a novelette. A whimsical monstrosity.

Now you know my trauma.
Now you know my story.
The kettle is on the stove.

.

THOUGHTS ON GRIEF
AND MENTAL
HEALTH

"Healing isn't linear."

— R.F. VIRDI

WAITING FOR TEA
(OR, A REFLECTION ON GRIEF)

OCTOBER 22, 2018

T his past Thursday (October 18, 2018) my mother passed away after a three-month battle with leukemia. When I got the call from my father I fell into a strange sort of catharsis, the kind that consists of a) sadness over the loss of my mother and b) the emotional release brought by knowing that she can finally rest, free of the horror of cancer. I thought I could get on with life, with some differences of course, but wow: that first night, that first day after she'd passed...

That night I went and bought a bottle of Glenlivet to sip while my friends came over to hangout and watch Netflix with me. What I did not anticipate, however, was gradually pouring glass after glass from about 10:00 p.m. until about 8:00 a.m., proceeding to get zero sleep whatsoever, and then attempt to go into work for an eight-hour shift the following morning, two minutes into which the ladies in the back office sent me home because I was definitely not in any condition to be working.

I was in shock.

So I went home and proceeded to sleep for about eight hours before meeting my dad for dinner at my mother's favorite Chinese restaurant. We had some great food, a couple of drinks and talked about what we remembered most about mom, about the legacy she'd left behind. My mother was someone who helped a lot of people throughout her life; she cared about people, went out of her way to make sure they were getting along in their lives. She was also the co-founder of Major Impact Theater, a nonprofit theater group for adults with disabilities, and I am so amazed and proud of the profound effect she had on all of those actors' lives. She helped them come out of their shells, and they are now some of the most outgoing people I have ever met. And my mother is a big reason why.

I think my coping started at that moment. I had said my goodbyes mentally a few days before, but the realization of reality began to sink in that night at dinner. And I knew that while it was perfectly okay to feel said, I didn't want to wallow in that misery--mom wouldn't have wanted that of us.

Grief affects people differently, though grief itself is something universally understood. Things I've tried to be more proactive about in these last few days, weeks, and months, really are meditating everyday. I find that if I can focus myself early in the morning that I'm usually good to go for the rest of the day.

I've gotten into a sleep schedule that doesn't involve going to be at 2:00 a.m. anymore.

I make sure to keep a notebook on hand most

of the time for jotting down story ideas, or to just write down a thought I'm having.

I'm working on getting back into my gym routine.

I'm reading more.

I'm breathing more.

I'm learning to appreciate life and the people in my life more than I have before.

I have my moments where I allow myself to cry. It's healthy, and it's important to not hold that in. It's important to let myself grieve when it comes.

Coping is not easy, but it is certainly possible. You just have to take it day by day.

I WROTE this almost four years ago. Things have changed. I have changed. Things feel a bit… bleak; I have a lot I'm going through personally.

A theme my writing always seems to come back to is grief and its relationship with hope, and that has been most apparent in my last two books—*The World Breaker Requiem* and *A Cup of*

Tea at the Mouth of Hell. They're very different from each other, in content and in length (*Requiem* is a novel whereas *A Cup of Tea* barely registers as a novelette), but what brings them together is the commentary on personal loss. For me, that loss is my mother.

To expand, *Requiem* was a general meditation on the loss of a parent. *A Cup of Tea* is an absolute metaphor, with Light and the tea kettle acting interchangeably. I have felt empty for four years; I have been searching for comfort, for a way to fill that emptiness. But it's tough, and I haven't exactly figured it out yet—and that's okay. In writing *A Cup of Tea* I tackled some extremely heavy subject matter and I addressed pieces of my past I thought I'd left behind. In doing so, I realized I have a lot to work on personally. In doing so, I put the kettle on the stove, as it were.

Now, I'm just waiting for the water to boil.

I'm just waiting for my tea.

Self-Expectations and Load Management

Fuck it. I'm a mess. My thoughts are everywhere and nowhere. Half the time it's hard for me to concentrate; my anxiety and my depression are the biggest roadblocks in my life—*I* am the biggest roadblock in my life. The bullshit starts in the center of my mind and worms through the rest of me; my fears poison me and affect the way I perceive reality and the people in my life.

I am a good person, but I am sick with fear and I've been a fucking wreck since October 18,

2018. Death has a way of doing that. But I've been scared for a while—I've been scared since I was a child. It took years for me to learn empathy, for me to say I fucking love you to the people in my life.

I am a good person. I am a good person. How many times do I have to say it before I kill the voices in my head, before I make this fucking parasite go away? Hell is a place of one's own making, and I've been living in a mental inferno for more than two years. I have been ugly, I have been emotionally abusive, and I have been so absolutely self-absorbed. My fear poisoned me and it made me poison people whom I love.

I am a good person, but I've been an ugly one as well, and I have punished myself unrelentingly for my actions. Punished myself, dug deeper and deeper and buried myself in a pit because I was afraid to look at myself in the mirror and stare at the monster inside. Because I was afraid to admit that things were not okay and that I *needed* to change.

I am not my thoughts, but my thoughts are me—*were me*, are parasitic echoes and relics clinging desperately, intent on destroying me from the inside out.

Enough. Fuck that. I am a good person, and I am not my thoughts.

It's hard to write this, but it was even harder to first admit all of this to myself. It was hard to look into the abyss and watch it grin. To comprehend my shadow twin was destroying me from the inside out. These last almost-three years have been filled with so much joy, but my sorrow was so profound it was almost impossible for me to see it. I lost my mom, I lost my mind. I gained a wife and children, but I almost let my vultures swallow me, devour me and steal it all away.

The guilt will always call you back if you let it. The vultures will pick at the corpse of your mind if you keep punishing yourself. *We* are responsible for ourselves, for internal change. I am a puzzle and I'm intent on solving myself.

The Drug in Me is Me

S ometimes we unwittingly seek misery to feel alive—to remind us we're alive. At least, that's the way it works for me whether I fucking want it to or not. I am Depression; sometimes I get high as fuck on the most illogical of anxieties. It's a bit of a vicious circle, and I often times have trouble figuring out just where the hell it starts.

Depression just is, but it's exacerbated by anxiety, and boy do I have a lot of that. Social. Professional. Often times the two go hand-in-hand. I overthink everything; I ruminate more than is healthy. Did I say something wrong? Did my joke come across? Am I a good writer? Jesus fuck, why did I think this was a good idea? Hey, I'm sorry if... I'm sorry about... Fuck. No one likes you. Yeah, people are busy and responses aren't instant, that's logical, but you're also a self-righteous, self-important fuck. Your humor sucks and everyone knows the self-deprivation is a shitty attempt to self-brand.

Look. That guy—that dude above? Fuck him. You have issues—everyone does. But you're trying. You always try, and no one can take that from you. We all have our deficits, we all have our strengths.

Right. I know. But what if—?

What if?

Then what?

Why the fuck?

Triple A—Anticipate, Agonize, Accept. Anticipate your current and your imminent failures; agonize over them; accept yourself for the failure that you are.

Repeat.

Repeat.

Repeat.

Hey, look, a dog. Gonna tell my wife—

But what if I'm annoying her?

Rewind. Four years ago. You just bought a house. Three bedrooms. You have your own office. But wait—fuck. You're going to have kids one day, and then you'll have to turn the guest room into the nursery, and you'll have to turn the office into the guest room, so—fuck it. Let's just move our desk into the master bedroom so we don't have to worry about that later.

Now you don't have an office. Where the fuck are you going to work in peace? Sh_t.

Stop. Make too many covers for your book. Change them. Agonize over the inconsistency and the myriad "editions" no on goodreads; why the fuck can't you delete old covers?

Stupid author. Stupid OCD.

Commence a week of ruminating on the changes.

Exhausted.

Happy.

Fuck, I write slow. I'm inconsistent. _ have a

million things to my agenda but if I don't put something out this year then people will forget about me, about my books—

Hardcovers!

Beyond exhausted. Losing sleep.

Repeat steps one through five, where every the hell they start, whatever the hell they are.

Hey, sorry I'm depressed. I'll try to be happier so you don't ignore...me.

Feel that needle in your skin. The adrenaline manifested by the anticipation of clarity.

Sorry. I've been busy. I've been dealing with my own depression.

Yeah. I get it. Totally understand. I've been going through a lot of that myself. I'm doing better, thanks, and I'm glad to hear you are as well.

But...

Please...

Fine. Give me the syringe.

Channeling Trauma

I n August 2018, just four months after I had gotten married, my mother was abruptly diagnosed with leukemia.

On October 18, 2018, in the autumn dusk, she passed away, and I have carried that trauma ever since.

My mother was my biggest fan, as a writer and a son. She never got to see me become a father, and it pains me that my daughters will never know her aside from pictures and oral recollections.

By now you might be wondering how any of this is relevant. Fear not, baby goats, and buckle for the introspective journey that is the story of how *The World Breaker Requiem* came to be.

The original plan for this book was much different than the book that eventually made it to publication. Originally, it was an alternate universe recreation of my novel Vultures. Similar in some ways, but more or less an examination of how many ways the life of a man could go wrong. I planned for a November 2021 release, but as the date drew closer it was clear nothing about this endeavor was feasible—so I pulled the plug and had a long think.

As some of you might know, and as most of you undoubtedly do not (and this is not a dig at your intelligence; I just have the tendency to ramble points of conversation into fucking oblivion), I am adopted. I was born in Romania in August 1990; by January 1991 (I think) I was living with my adoptive parents in Brooklyn, New York.

"That's great, Luke, but what the hell does this have to do with your book?"

When I sat down to continue working out the massive fucking kinks in *Requiem*, I decided I wanted to exam the mindset of a man adopted as a boy whose relationship with his adoptive mother devolved over the years. What kind of feelings would this conjure? What kind of reactions? The more I thought about it, the deeper I got into my own head, and the further into writing the first act, I realized, lo and behold, the primary theme of the book.

Let me ask you a question. Would that you could, regardless of potential negative consequences a la the butterfly effect, would you go back in time to rectify a moment of pain? I thought about this a countless number of times, boozed up in a bathtub many a nights with my phone as I stumbled through the story.

Each of the primary characters (all of the characters, really) are struggling with this very question as they soldier on through a bleak world made bleaker by the loss of loved ones. Secondary to this was the relationship between mother and child and the way this impacted the way the characters reacted to the world at large.

I wrote the epilogue to *The World Breaker Requiem* several months before I wrote the final chapter and it serves its purpose well, acting as the finish line and accompanying red ribbon to a fucking marathon of misery. I wrote this book in the midst of a pandemic, during undoubtedly the toughest year and a half of my life, and getting to read that epilogue after having written the final chapter was a fucking breath of fresh air. An exhalation of a breath I didn't know that I'd been holding. Finishing The World Breaker Requiem was the awakening I needed, that moment of catharsis and the clarity to realize that I'd not been okay for a long time.

But I'm better now as of writing this. So much better mentally, emotionally, and physically. *The World Breaker Requiem* is the most difficult piece of fiction I've ever written, primarily because it's not entirely fiction. But it's also the most important.

It saved me.

About the Author

Luke Tarzian was born in Bucharest, Romania. His parents made the extremely poor choice of adopting him less than six months into his life. As such, he's resided primarily in the United States and currently lives in California. Somehow, his twin daughters tolerate him.

Unfortunately, he can also be found online and, to the dismay of his clients, also functions as a cover artist for independent authors.